A Princess Tail

By Uri Sperling

Illustrated by Jodine Aidyl Suyko

Edited by Charlotte Nusberg & Emily Costanze

Published in the United States by Sperling LLC

First (and probably last) Edition 10/2017

ISBN-13: 978-0-692-93876-8

Please send feedback/comments to sperling@gmail.com

Just one of our silly bed time stories.

Inspired by Liv, Nina and Aimee.

Zoey Sparkle was the nicest princess anyone had ever met.

She was kind and beautiful and if you've met her, you would never ever forget.

Zoey just loved to dance and of course do all sorts of magical princess stuff.

But helping others was her favorite part, and she would never get enough.

But this is not just another ordinary princess tale.

Our lovely princess had a secret, our princess had a tail!

She was seriously embarrassed, she was indeed ashamed.

If people find out, they might not like her, she was really kind of scared.

Princess Zoey was hoping there was a magic spell,
a spell that could help her get rid of her silly tail.

So one day she decided it was way overdue
to visit the Wizard as he might have a clue.

How to make a princess tail disappear,
he must know she thought, that is fairly clear.

And the wizard was quite astonished at first look,
but then he opened up his magic spells book.

He quickly turned to the 'tail spells' on page 369,

and read how to get rid of a tail attached to a princess behind.

The spell was quite simple the wizard thought,
he whispered "hocus pocus" as he spread some salt.

He waved his wand high, he whispered the secret spell,
it's going to work, he knew it, he could tell.

A little explosion and some green smoke,
and what a shock, the princess's tail...started to talk.

And the wizard cried, "Hey, it's not my fault",
"Maybe I need to add just a little bit more salt."

And so he waved the magic wand again up high,
and shouted the magic spell in order to tell the tail bye-bye.

But this time what a surprise,
our friendly talking tail, now suddenly had eyes.

"Oh no", the wizard yelled "this tail is bewitched",
And out of the blue the wizard simply ditched.

And sweet Zoey again stared at her lively tail,

which came to life thanks to that spell.

"Well hello" said the tail, not missing a beat,
"I'm really hungry, I would like to eat".

And the little tail was hungry all right,
he wanted to eat all day and all night.

He was a hungry talking tail from the moment he woke,
Our friendly funny tail was seriously no joke.

Our princess thought it was quite a mess,

she said, "Please keep hiding under my dress".

"As long as you quietly down there keep,
i will give you whatever you want to eat".

But then one day at a festive parade,
the tail couldn't resist and out he glanced.

He looked at the dancers, and listened to the trumpeters,
enjoying the music, he even joined in the cheers.

When suddenly one of the kids started to yell,

"Hey everybody, look, the princess has a tail!".

The music stopped and everyone stared,

the tail was surprised, the princess ashamed.

The camera man, a picture he took,

for tomorrow's newspaper he thought, everyone would want
to take a look.

And our princess ran to her castle room to hide,

she closed the door and obviously cried.

She cried all night and the tail was sad,
he really didn't mean at all to be bad.

But by the morning the princess wasn't that mad,
she found a newspaper right next to her bed.

And on the cover was herself and of course her tail,
and the princess in the picture looked, well kind of pale.

And the headline was bold and it wasn't small,
It said, "Our princess has the most awesome tail of all."

And our sweet Zoey couldn't believe her eyes,

she now thought that hiding her tail may have not been so wise.

And so out of her room she quietly went,

she sat on the castle wall and to her amazement,

all the kids in the kingdom without a fail,

They all had made themselves beautiful tails.

And the tail was happy, the princess too,

it was a beautiful day, I swear this story is true.

And so this tale about a tail and a magic spell, was

an extraordinary princess story we just had to tell,

about a secret so deep, that no one would believe,

but when it was out the princess was totally relieved.

So if a secret you tried so hard to hide is suddenly revealed,

you may feel sad and exposed, like you have lost your shield.

But you may be surprised that besides being sad,

you may actually feel relieved perhaps even glad.

So be yourself, be strong be true, no need to feel so frail,
because there are some gloomy moments in every fairytale.

Your future is bright, just smile and set your sail,
even if you happen to have a secret, magic talking tail.

Made in the USA
Lexington, KY
17 April 2018